This book belongs to

. . . .

LADYBIRD BOOKS

UK | USA | Canada | Ireland | Australia | India | New Zealand | South Africa

Ladybird Books is part of the Penguin Random House group of companies
whose addresses can be found at global.penguinrandomhouse.com.

www.penguin.co.uk   www.puffin.co.uk   www.ladybird.co.uk

Penguin
Random House
UK

First published 2022
001

Licensed by

Printed in China

The authorized representative in the EEA is Penguin Random House Ireland,
Morrison Chambers, 32 Nassau Street, Dublin D02 YH68

A CIP catalogue record for this book is available from the British Library

ISBN: 978-0-241-54339-9

All correspondence to:
Ladybird Books, Penguin Random House Children's
One Embassy Gardens, 8 Viaduct Gardens, London SW11 7BW

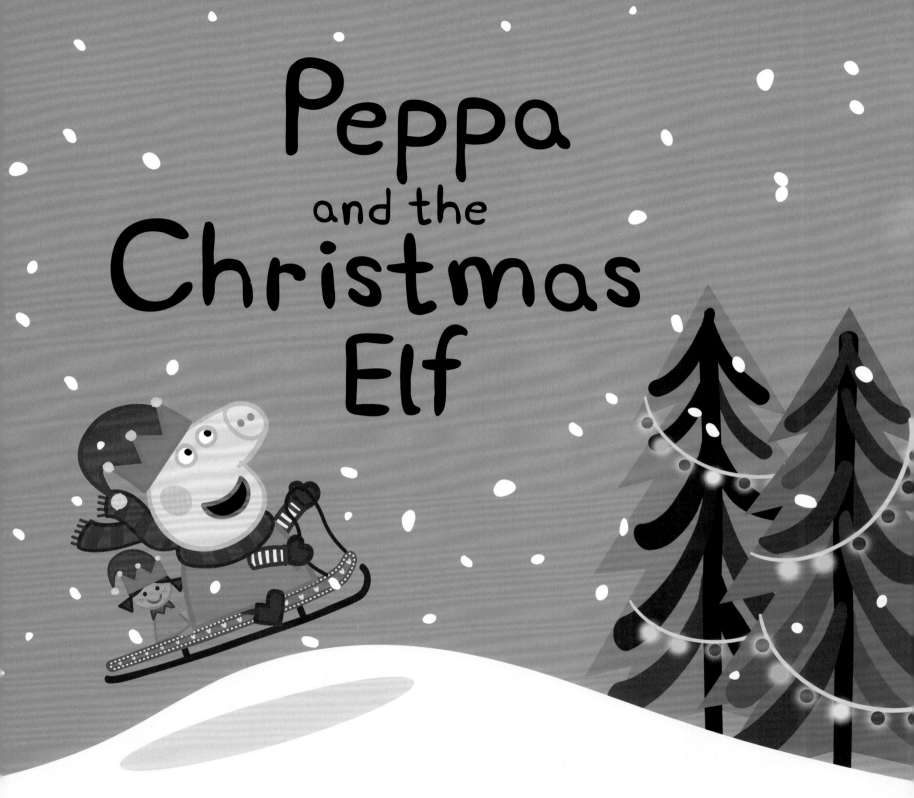

Peppa
and the
Christmas
Elf

It was Christmas Eve, and Peppa and George were making cookies for Santa with Granny and Grandpa Pig. "Are we being helpful?" asked Peppa, whipping the spoon around and getting mixture everywhere.

"Oh yes," said Grandpa Pig.
"You're *wonderful* helpers."
"We're like Santa's elves,
George," said Peppa.
George giggled. "Kiss-mas els!"

SPLODGE!

SPLAT!

"I wish I could meet an elf," said Peppa. "I bet they *love* adventures!"
"Yes," agreed Grandpa Pig.
Granny Pig told Peppa and George that, as they stirred the mixture, they could make a special Christmas wish.

"Kiss-mas dine-saw!" cried George.
"*Shh*, George," whispered Peppa. "You're not
supposed to tell anyone your wish."

George wished for a
Christmas dinosaur . . .

and Peppa
wished for an
adventure with
a Christmas elf!

Jingle! Jingle!

"Did you hear that?" asked Peppa.
"It was a jingle-ly sound coming from
outside. I think my wish has come true!"
"Shall we go and see?" said Granny Pig.

"Ahh, look at that," said Grandpa Pig when they got outside.
"There's an owl in the Christmas tree, jingling the bells."
"Oh," said Peppa, sighing. "That's not my Christmas wish."
"Never mind," said Granny Pig. "I'm sure you'll get your wish soon."

Just then, there was another sound . . .
"Ho! Ho! Ho!
Merry Christmas!"

Jingle!

Jingle!

Jingle!

"Daddy!" cheered Peppa and George.
Mummy and Daddy Pig had arrived to pick them up.
"Are you ready to ride the Christmas train?" said Daddy Pig.
"Yes!" cried Peppa and George.

"Have fun," said Granny Pig, waving goodbye. "We'll see you later for our **Christmas sleepover.**"

As Daddy Pig started the car's engine, Peppa spotted something red peeking out from behind a tree. "Look!" she cried, pointing. "A Christmas elf!"

Mummy Pig turned around. "Ahhh, it's a little robin," she said. "Santa has *lots* of elves," said Peppa. "They can't all be at his workshop, can they?"

"Probably not. Maybe you did see one," said Daddy Pig, winking. "Right, let's go to the Christmas train!"
"*Choo! Choo!*" cheered George.

When they arrived at the Christmas train platform, Peppa and George were *very* excited. The train was decorated with lots of twinkly fairy lights.

"All aboard the Christmas train!" Miss Rabbit called out.

"First stop – the Christmas helter-skelter!"

"Hooray!" everyone cheered.
"*Choo! Choo!*" said George.

At the helter-skelter, Peppa looked up and spotted a red hat in one of the windows. "Found you, Christmas elf!" she cried.

But when Mummy and Daddy Pig looked up, all they saw was Molly Mole wearing a little red hat. "Merry Christmas, Peppa!" cried Molly.
"Oh. Merry Christmas, Molly," replied Peppa.

Everyone had lots of helter-skelter fun, but soon it was time to move on. "Follow me to the Christmas Ferris wheel!" called Miss Rabbit.

Right at the very top of the Ferris wheel, Peppa spotted something in a little red hat. "Found you, Christmas elf!" she cried.

But when Mummy Pig looked, all she saw was Mr Bull wearing a little red hat!

At the gingerbread workshop, Peppa spotted the Christmas elf behind a gingerbread house. "Found you, Christmas elf!" said Peppa. "Look, Daddy!"

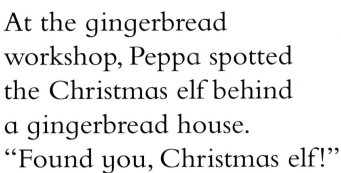

But when Daddy Pig looked, all he saw was a gingerbread house with a little red hat on top of it!

The final Christmas activity was the sledging hill.
As Daddy Pig and George whizzed off,
Peppa spotted the elf sledging, too.
"Follow that elf, Mummy!" she cried.

Wheeeee!

Peppa and Mummy Pig set off. Their sledge **raced** down the hill. The sledge was going so fast, Mummy Pig couldn't stop it. "Aaahhh!" she cried as the speeding sledge zoomed up into the air and landed . . .

Aaahhh!

. . . in a snow-elf! *Sploosh!*

"Who put *that* there?" said Mummy Pig, covered
head-to-toe in snow.

"It wasn't me, Mummy Pig," said Daddy Pig. "It must've
been the Christmas elf!"

SPLOOSH!

"Anyway, time to go," said Daddy Pig. "Granny
and Grandpa Pig will be waiting for us."
"Yippee!" cheered Peppa and George.

When Peppa and George got back to Granny
and Grandpa Pig's house, they put out some
cookies for Santa, and then got ready for bed.

Peppa told them all about her adventure with the elf.
"...But I didn't even get to talk to the elf," she said.
"Time to sleep, little ones," said Granny Pig. "May
all your Christmas wishes come true!"

But Peppa and George didn't hear ...
They were already fast asleep!

Very early on Christmas morning, Peppa and George ran in to wake Mummy and Daddy Pig.

Then they ran into Granny and Grandpa Pig's bedroom and woke them up, too!

They all headed downstairs to find Santa
had left presents for everyone!
"Kiss-mas dine-saw!" cheered George.
His Christmas wish had come true!

Suddenly, Peppa heard a sound.
Jingle! Jingle!
She looked up. Right at the top
of the tree was a toy . . .
"Christmas elf!" Peppa cried,
jumping up and down.

Peppa cuddled the Christmas elf. "Thank you for the adventure," she whispered. Peppa's Christmas wish had come true, too!
Mummy Pig took the elf's hat off and secretly put it on Daddy Pig's head.

"What's that?" asked Daddy Pig, reaching up and finding the hat. He looked over at Mummy Pig . . . "It wasn't me," said Mummy Pig, smiling. "It must've been the Christmas elf!"

Peppa loves her Christmas elf.
Everyone loves Peppa's Christmas elf!